The Cat at Night

by Dahlov Ipcar

Dahlov Ipcar came to love Maine while growing up in the 1920s, spending many summers along the coast with her parents, the famous artists William and Marguerite Zorach. She moved to Maine permanently in 1937 with her husband, Adolph, to live on a small farm in Georgetown.

The Little Fisherman, the very first children's book illustrated by Ipcar, was published in 1945. This wonderful book serves as a milestone in her now illustrious career; not only did it help establish her distinctive style, but it also ignited a four-decade creative run during which she wrote and illustrated more than thirty children's books. Her final book was My Wonderful Christmas Tree (1986), for which she drew inspiration from the woods and fields surrounding her beloved Maine farmhouse.

While Ipcar has not illustrated a new children's book since the 1980s, she remains a prolific artist in her nineties. Her work is now part of the permanent collections of a number of prestigious art institutions. In addition to painting, including a number of large-scale murals for public buildings in Maine and elsewhere, Ipcar has created hooked rugs, cloth sculptures, lithographs, and needlepoint tapestries.

Ipcar's fanciful, intricate artwork is known worldwide and she remains a Maine treasure.

Other books by Dahlov Ipcar

The Little Fisherman

Lobsterman

My Wonderful Christmas Tree

Brown Cow Farm

Hard Scrabble Harvest

For Goliath
cat extraordinary

Islandport Press
P.O. Box 10
Yarmouth, Maine 04096
books@islandportpress.com
www.islandportpress.com

The Cat at Night was first published in 1969 by Doubleday & Company. This edition
published in 2008 by Islandport Press in cooperation with Dahlov Ipcar.

Production Date: 01/19/11
Plant and Location: Printed by Everbest Printing Company, Ltd., Nansha, China
Job/Batch# 99198

ISBN: 978-1-934031-23-0
Library of Congress Control Number: 2008941434

The Cat at

ISLANDPORT  PRESS   YARMOUTH, MAINE

Night

by Dahlov Ipcar

When the farmer goes to bed, he winds the clock and he puts the cat out.

But what does the cat do out there in the darkness all night long?

Does he curl up on a chair on the porch and sleep all night?

No, he doesn't. The cat can see at night. The sky is dark and full of stars, but everything else is like day to him. He can see the dog sleeping in the doghouse and the doves asleep on the dovecote.

But the cat doesn't feel like sleeping. Night is the best time of all—the time when he likes to go exploring.

He goes walking softly through the blackness, and we can't see what is there. But the cat can see as clear as day. What do you think he sees?

He sees the flowers with all their different shapes.
And he sees the big soft-winged moths that fly in the
night—like the butterflies that fly in the daytime.

Where do you think the cat is walking now?

He is walking through the henhouse, where all the hens are sleeping. They are dreaming dreams, fast asleep on their roosts.

The cat walks quietly through, looking for a rat to catch.

Where do you think he is now?

He is down behind the barn, where the big farm truck and the tractor are parked.

And where do you think the cat is walking now?

He is walking through the fields, where the cows are sleeping under the apple trees.

He is walking underneath a big white horse, who is fast asleep standing up. That is the way that horses usually sleep.

The cat walks through the night fields. Now he is hunting.
But what is he hunting for?

He is hunting for rabbits in the vegetable garden.

The cat is walking through the dark woods now.
We can see the black trees, but what can he see that
we don't see?

He can see all the animals that live in the woods. They are all wide awake, too, because they feel safe in the nighttime. The deer are browsing and the foxes are hunting. There are owls in the trees, and a family of skunks is out for a walk.

The cat walks along the road to the nearby town.
All the cars and trucks that pass on the road shine
their lights on him, and his eyes shine back at them.
But what else does he see on the way to town?

He can see the road
without lights. He can see
it just as it looks in the
daytime. And he can see
the edges of the road, where
a raccoon family is hunting
for frogs in the ditch.

And when he reaches the town, what does he find?

He finds other cats there waiting for him. They all go prowling together through the back streets and over the rooftops among the chimney pots. Sometimes they fight with each other, and sometimes they sing cat songs together—mournful, sweet, wailing songs—the kind that only cats like.

When the dawn comes, he leaves his friends and walks
back home down the road, through misty, morning fields,
where horses are awake and grazing and butterflies
are flying about among the flowers.

He walks slowly back to the white farmhouse,
for he is tired after his long night.

He arrives at the kitchen door right after the cows have been milked—just in time for breakfast.

And the farmer's wife says, "Good morning, kitty. Did you have a good night's sleep?"

But the cat only yawns a wide cat yawn and drinks his milk.

Then he curls up in the big armchair by the stove and falls sound asleep, purring to himself. And the farmer says, "What a lazy cat. He sleeps all night and he sleeps all day, too!" But the cat doesn't hear him. He is dreaming about all his adventures in the long, wonderful, dark night.